McKenzi B.

Blue Bear Finds a Rainbow

BLUE BEAR FINDS A RAINBOW
Copyright © 2011 McKenzie Leigh Betts

ISBN 978-1-886068-51-3
Library of Congress Control Number: 2011937413

Published by Fruitbearer Publishing, LLC
P.O. Box 777, Georgetown, DE 19947
302.856.6649 • FAX 302.856.7742
www.fruitbearer.com • info@fruitbearer.com

Illustrated by Stacie Desautels
Graphic design and editing by Candy Abbott

Printed in the United States of America
by BookMasters, Inc.
30 Amberwood Parkway, Ashland, OH 44805
January 2012 • Job #M9168

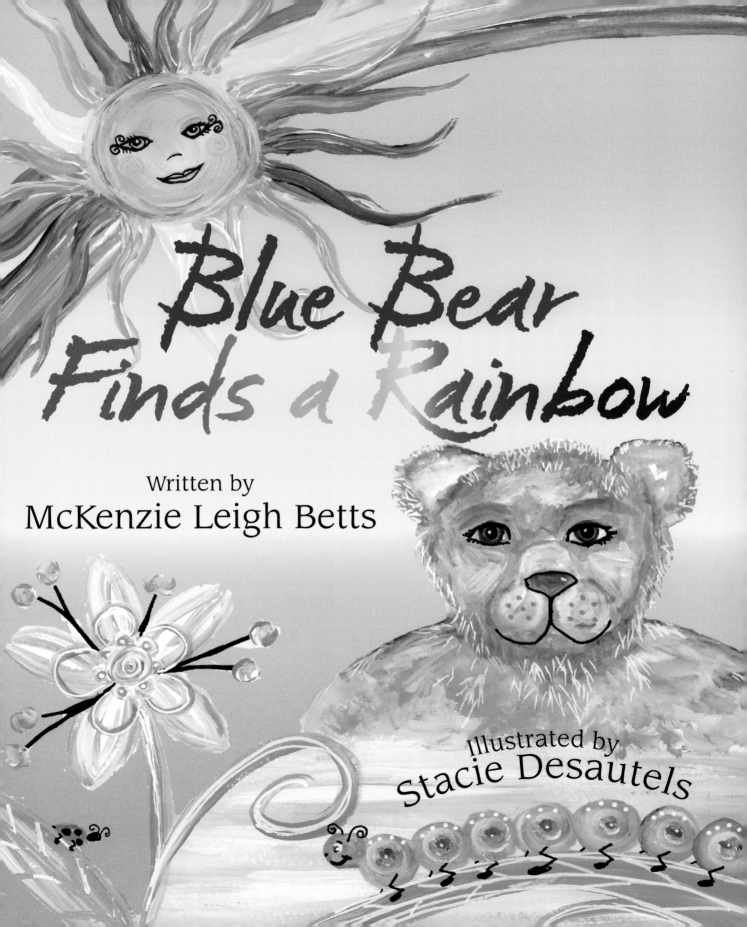

Blue Bear Finds a Rainbow

Written by
McKenzie Leigh Betts

Illustrated by
Stacie Desautels

Once upon a time there was a Blue Bear.

He always wanted to know why he was blue, but he never figured it out.

He was sad because he did not fit in with all the other bears.

"You look so weird and ugly," Bully Bear said.

Blue Bear decided he must be weird and ugly.

Blue Bear was always by himself. He had no friends at all. Oh, how he wished that someday he could have a friend.

Then, one day, Blue Bear walked down a dirt path. He thought he had bad luck because—guess what?—it started to rain, and he got all wet.

But Blue Bear kept walking, walking, walking, until the sun began to peek through the raindrops.

"A rainbow!" Blue Bear yelled with joy.

But nobody heard.

Blue Bear thought for a minute. *Maybe this is why I'm blue.*

But somebody did hear him!

"Don't be sad, Blue Bear," the rainbow said. "You can go to the end of the rainbow and make a wish."

"Can I wish to not be blue?" Blue Bear asked.

"Of course you can," the rainbow smiled.

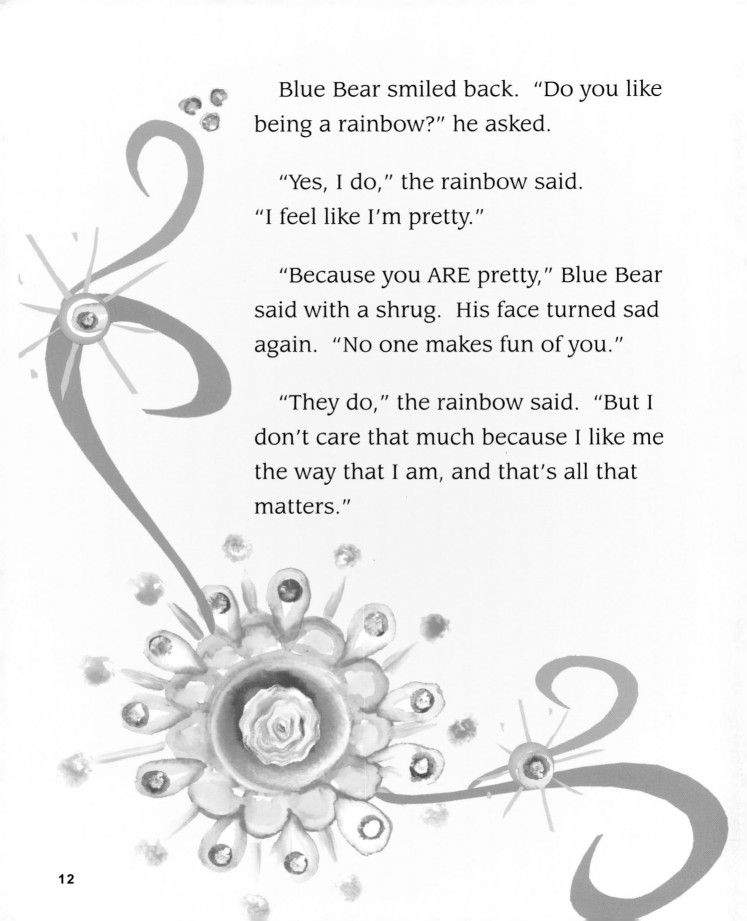

Blue Bear smiled back. "Do you like being a rainbow?" he asked.

"Yes, I do," the rainbow said. "I feel like I'm pretty."

"Because you ARE pretty," Blue Bear said with a shrug. His face turned sad again. "No one makes fun of you."

"They do," the rainbow said. "But I don't care that much because I like me the way that I am, and that's all that matters."

Blue Bear started walking again to find the end of the rainbow. He walked and walked and walked. And, sure enough, he finally found the end of the rainbow.

Blue Bear was very happy, because he could make a wish to not be blue.

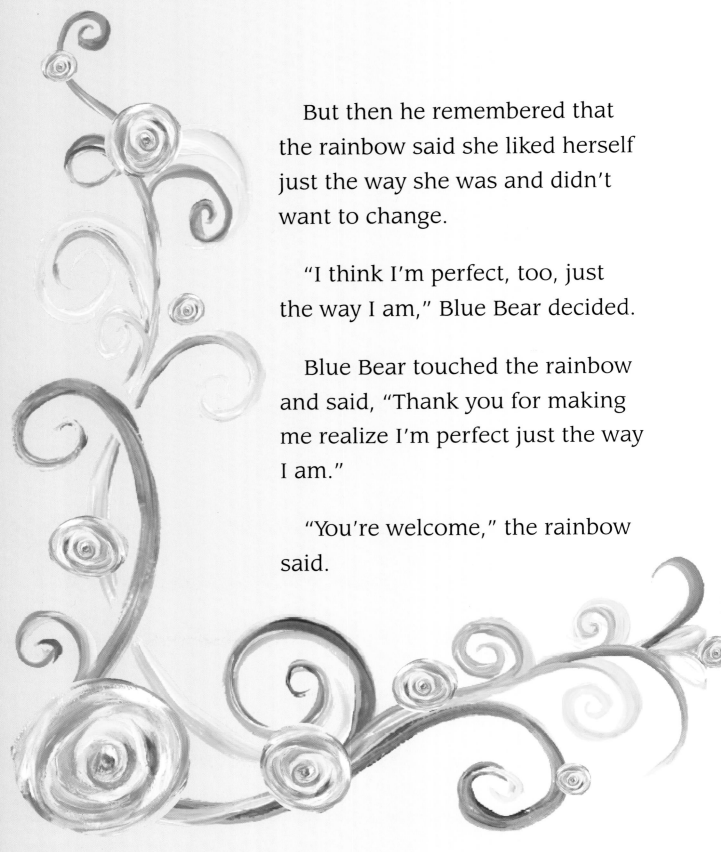

But then he remembered that the rainbow said she liked herself just the way she was and didn't want to change.

"I think I'm perfect, too, just the way I am," Blue Bear decided.

Blue Bear touched the rainbow and said, "Thank you for making me realize I'm perfect just the way I am."

"You're welcome," the rainbow said.

Blue Bear giggled. "I don't need to change," he said. "All I need to do is talk to people, and they will talk to me, and I will have friends."

The rainbow looked concerned. "You know, Blue Bear, not everybody is as smart or as nice as you are."

Blue Bear began to worry again. "What can I do about that?" he asked.

For a long time, the rainbow thought and thought. Then she smiled a big, rainbow smile and said, "Be nice to them anyway!"

The rainbow and Blue Bear both lived happily ever after.

Oh, and Blue Bear made lots and lots of friends!

The End

Rainbow Reflections

- Have you ever not felt good about yourself?

  If so, what happened to make you feel bad?

- Did you learn anything from *Blue Bear* or *the Rainbow* about how to act if you do not like who you are or how you look?

  If so, what did you learn?

- What can you do if you know of someone who is not happy with himself or herself?

- Has anyone ever made fun of you because you might look or act different?

  If so, how did you handle it?

- If someone made fun of you now, after reading *Blue Bear Finds a Rainbow,* how do you think you would react?

- Have you ever made fun of someone because they looked or acted different?

  If so, why? Would you do it again?

Meet the Author

McKenzie Leigh Betts wrote *Blue Bear Finds a Rainbow* just for fun when she was nine years old. Her parents, Bobby and Dianne, were so impressed with the moral of the story that they wanted to share it with others.

McKenzie is such a fun loving girl who loves to laugh and simply enjoy life. She is very active and is a member of the YMCA swim team. McKenzie enjoys going to school to learn new things as well as to be with her friends. McKenzie's friends are very special to her; she loves to spend as much time as she can with them. Family time is an important part of life and since she travels for swim and her brother, Ryan, travels for ice hockey, there is plenty of time together on the road as a family. McKenzie dreams of being a teacher when she grows up, she would love to teach grade school, so whenever she can she likes to play teacher at home.

We hope you enjoy McKenzie's story and can learn a valuable lesson from it.

Meet the Illustrator

Stacie Desautels is the colorful, whimsical artist of Daisy DeZigns Art Studio in Salisbury, Maryland. Her style is fresh and full of swirling colors designed to delight the viewer. A two-time breast cancer survivor, Desautels has a true appreciation for the magical moments and miracles that occur every day. Stacie recognizes her talent and passion for painting as a gift from God, the Master Artist, to be used to touch hearts and inspire changed lives. Desautels is known for her eccentric illustrations created for the Wicomico County Autumn Wine Festival each year, numerous children's murals, and her *Mindful Moments:* inspirational "Thought for the Day" cards. Stacie's artwork reflects her optimistic outlook on life: colorful, whimsical, happy art that she hopes will evoke peace, joy, and gratitude. Visit Stacie at www.daisydezignsartstudio.com or all 443.783.9518.

To Order This Book

Blue Bear Finds a Rainbow is available from your favorite bookstore or from Amazon and other distributors.

For autographed books, please include the name(s) you want inscribed. Send your name, address, phone number, and e-mail (if applicable), with $15.00 per book + $7.00 S/H to:

The Betts Family
P.O. Box 110
Lincoln, DE 19960

Please make checks payable to McKenzie Betts.
Questions? E-mail mcryan4@comcast.net

For bulk order discounts
call 302.856.6649 or e-mail info@fruitbearer.com

www.fruitbearer.com